"*I was deeply moved by Robert ....g and* **Indeterminate Perambulation.** *It is a brilliant meditation on life and death, on the essence of our shared humanity and on our shared fate. Elegantly written and utterly original, this book will surely endure.*"
Robert Olen Butler, Pulitzer Prize-winning author of *A Good Scent from a Strange Mountain*

"*This novella is heartfelt and utterly beautiful, yet grounded in strength, integrity, and conviction. Robert McGowan takes his readers for walks in the neighborhood, and along the way talks about art and writing, religion and philosophy, life, death, and dying. Wise remarks about everything important in this world. Wisdom cast as fiction. McGowan at his very best.*"
Christine Cote, Founder, Shanti Arts; Editor and Publisher, *Still Point Arts Quarterly* and *Stone Voices*

About McGowan's *NAM: Things That Weren't True and Other Stories* :
"***Robert McGowan displays remarkable range and depth.***"
Stewart O'Nan, eminent American novelist and editor of the anthology, *The Vietnam Reader*

"*I am a fan of McGowan's work because, even when it's impossible to know from your own experience whether a story is factually accurate, you know very well that the story is true, really true. That's great writing.*"
Carol Brightman, author of *Writing Dangerously: Mary McCarthy and Her World* (National Book Critics Circle Award) and, with the renowned artist Larry Rivers, of *Drawings and Digressions* (American Book Award)

About McGowan's *Happy Again at Last: Life in the Art World* :
"***McGowan speaks of the art world in a deeply engaging and distinctive voice . . . all of it feels absolutely true to me.***"
Janet Koplos, Contributing Editor, *Art in America*

A LONG AND INDETERMINATE
PERAMBULATION

Copyright © 2012 Robert McGowan

ISBN: 978-1-291-00919-4

A Long and Indeterminate Perambulation **is a work of fiction.**
Any likeness to any person living or dead is entirely coincidental.

10 9 8 7 6 5 4 3 2 1
First Printing

Design and Cover Art © 2012 Steve Hussy

For all queries contact:
Meridian Star Press,
29 Alpha Road, Gorleston, Norfolk. NR31 0LQ
United Kingdom

Meridian Star Press are:
Steve Hussy and Richard White

Published by Meridian Star Press 2012
www.murderslim.com/meridianstarpress.html

Printed and bound in the UK by the MPG Books Group,
Bodmin and King's Lynn

a *Long* and *Indeterminate Perambulation*
in the
Shadowy Realms
of
Life, Death, War, Art
and
Prescribed Exercise

by

Robert McGowan

Also by Robert McGowan:

NAM: Things That Weren't True And Other Stories
Meridian Star Press

Stories From The Art World
Thumbnail Press

Happy Again at Last: Life in the Art World
Shanti Arts Publishers, forthcoming 2013

South Main Stories
Meridian Star Press, forthcoming 2013

This book is for
Peg

With gratitude to

Jim Johnson

and to

Bert Sharpe

A Long and Indeterminate Perambulation is the lead story in the author's in-progress short fiction collection, *Old People*.

A Long and Indeterminate Perambulation

■ ■ ■

October 7, 2009

For a few years, until she disappeared only some weeks ago, I would watch from my front porch, where in pleasant weather I often sit to read, a really quite elderly woman, obviously infirm, shuffling along on her daily walks. I would see her pass at halting, deliberate gait, travel only a block or so up the street, and then pass by again, ever slowly, on her return home about a block away in the other direction. I always observed with poignant fascination how her little mutt, on a leash beside her, ambled along at a stride unnaturally slow and measured for a dog, as though the animal were consciously and sympathetically pacing itself so to accommodate its frail caretaker and fellow traveler.

Although I often waved to this woman and, on those occasions when she noticed my wave, she would wave back, I never spoke with her or knew her name. I have no knowledge of what has happened to her and her obliging pet, whether the woman has at last become too feeble to continue her exercise, whether she's at home or perhaps in a care facility, or whether she's now dead.

I remember surmising that this lady's walks, which, judging from her facial expression, did not appear to be pleasurable for her, had been prescribed by her physician as an aid to her staying alive yet a little while longer.

A Long and Indeterminate Perambulation

My own doctor, whom I've been seeing for nearly thirty years and whom I've for a very long time addressed by his first name, Jeffery, or sometimes Dr. Jeffery in order now and then to assure him respectfully that I'm mindful he's my doctor and not simply an old friend, has lately insisted that I too begin walking. Though I should say *resume* walking, because until recently I'd walked a couple of miles or more on three or four days of each week, for good health. And for pleasure as well; I for a very long time enjoyed continually renewing my acquaintance with this charming and comforting, and appealingly modest, neighborhood by means of my constitutionals from one end of it to another. It's true however that I have for a long while now neglected my walks, this for no particular reason I can bring to mind just now, but only because I've been, I suppose, neglectful. And perhaps also because of my painting, with which I am these days deeply preoccupied and which has lately required quite a good deal of concentration and energy, possibly in truth a little more than, in this my old age, I can give it with as much natural ease as I have previously. I'm seventy-five. Not so terribly old nowadays, though I was once, only moments ago it seems, very, very much younger.

So I suppose that now, on doctor's orders, as most likely was so of her as well, I will take the place of that enfeebled lady who once, with apparent reluctance, so regularly strode past my little house. And I will be doing so for the same reason she did, to perhaps extend my life somewhat beyond where it might end were I to remain wholly sedentary. Unexercised, as it were.

And I suppose further that those I'll pass by, my neighbors sitting on their porches, maybe reading, will think of me as I thought of her, as old and feeble and pitiful. Though I will take care that my expression not be as dour as hers. I will make sure it reveals I'm instead having a pleasant time, as mostly I will be, however pensive on various occasions might be my mood. The last thing I'd want is to darken anyone's afternoon leisure-time porch-sitting experience.

And I've decided also, as you see, to begin recording here in this notebook—and I will do this by date, because I want what I say here to be a tether to real life and to real days—I will record here some of the thoughts, my wandering ruminations, that happen to mind as I move along down these streets I've known so well for so long. I'm hopeful that both the walking and the writing will do me good. I will undertake both activities in the hope they will help me hold to the world, that they will keep me from fragmenting during this time, which feels to me like unreality, now that Adam has gone.

I want here in the beginning to enter a few essential points of information about Adam, in order that, should these pages survive, then so will he, or some small part of him, for a while, by way of these words.

My husband and my friend, Adam, a deeply sensitive and kind man concerned never to do ill to any living creature in this world or to any part of this world that harbors us, had a smile that would melt the devil's frigid heart. He was as consummately gentle a soul as anyone on this earth has ever known.

Yet as a young man, a boy really, decades before we met— he was eighteen years old—Adam joined the military. In 1950, I think. The Army. An uncle had persuaded him that a career in armed defense of his country would be as honorable and as well-spent a life as any he might choose to live.

He was sent to Korea in the last months of that war, in 1952.

And he would never tell me all of what he'd done and seen there. "I don't want to give further voice," I distinctly remember his saying, "to evils that have already found in me a place I should never have allowed them to occupy."

But he did write about those evils, converting experience to fiction. And he was a fine writer. Because he was in fact far better at writing than at self-promotion, Adam was seldom published, seeing to print only a handful of his stories in a handful of minor college literary journals.

Adam ended his relationship with the U.S. Army soon after his return from the war. He went to school and became a counselor, which is how we met many years later in 1970, at the university, he counseling students, helping them decide what to do with their lives, I a teacher in the art department.

We were together for thirty-eight years, married for thirty-six. No children. We'd married when Adam was nearly forty and I was only a couple of years younger. Middle age really. Too late in life for kids.

Even though I've lived by now for a bit more than seventy-five years, I think of my life before Adam as only a kind of prelude to the life we had together.

October 8, 2009

It occurred to me to wonder today, as I stepped off my porch to begin my walk, how many times I've seen the ends of rain. We'd had steady sprinkling all day long. I'd imagined having to report sheepishly to Dr. Jeffery that I'd sat out another twenty-four hours unexercised. But at last the rain ended and the sun abruptly reappeared, dramatically, the world bright again. I remember as a child waiting in our house for rains to end so that I could be outside. I don't recall what my thoughts were then as I waited, how melancholy they were or how untroubled. I do know that I've always felt soothed by the tender quiet of rainy days. I feel enveloped in them. And reflective, more reflective even than usual.

Although I've frequently varied my course on these walks around my neighborhood, my typical route, which I've measured to be about two miles, has been to walk from my house at 5617 Walker Avenue, east to Cooper Street, then north all the way to Central Avenue, where I turn west and walk to Lynndale, which takes me back to Walker. There I turn east again, in which direction sits my house—and how it saddens me now to say *my* house, not *our* house —second on my right. Or sometimes, though seldom—and why I've only so seldom reversed my course, I have no idea whatsoever —I've traveled this same route in the opposite direction. But, whichever direction I've taken, when I've strayed from the route I've described here I've generally expanded it to include two or three blocks farther in one direction and fewer in the opposite so that I've traveled approximately the same roughly two miles in either case, or I've cut my walk shorter by somewhere turning sooner so to take a shortcut back home. Or sometimes I take in an additional few blocks, making my walk not shorter but longer than usual. It varies. And by varying my walks I've over the years come to feel quite at home in every nook of this neighborhood. This the world I inhabit.

A Long and Indeterminate Perambulation

And that I have inhabited, as I've said, happily. In great comfort. Psychologically, I mean, emotionally. Aesthetically even. This is as utterly ordinary and wholly genuine a middle-class residential neighborhood as might be discovered in any city anywhere. And these are the qualities I warm to here. Adam and I lived for a few years in a downtown district of this city but felt increasingly out of place as the area grew increasingly hip and cool, as has become the hip and cool way to put it: "hip and cool." Hip and cool and glib and silly. We'd never imagined ourselves remotely either hip or cool. How laughable the thought that we'd ever been that or could be. And we always endeavored never to be glib, though we did admittedly on occasion lapse into silly. We'd moved downtown into, yes, a spectacularly raw and spacious loft, back when property in the district was inexpensive. I had a truly luxurious studio space, all the square feet I could use, high ceilings, perfect lighting, and I was near the city's best galleries in an area of downtown just beyond our own. The gallery that represents me, and has for . . . I think it's twenty-eight years now, was an easy walking distance away, The Duval Gallery. My devoted dealer, whom I thank here: Raymond Duval. There existed in those early days in the district a large population of artists, and also a large number of small businesses—printing companies, storage facilities, wholesalers of various sorts, a couple of plumbing companies, and the like— including the people who owned and operated these businesses and had done so there in the district for many years, decades even. Now that the district has become hip and cool, it's occupied mostly by clever little restaurants and clothing boutiques, mostly rather expensive, and quite a few rather bad galleries selling quite a lot of rather bad art to people who don't know any better than to buy it. And of course real estate is now wholly unaffordable down there for anyone of modest means, which makes it certainly unaffordable for most artists, but who by and large no longer want to be there anyway because of its phony-baloney hipness and coolness. Adam and I sold out fairly early and moved here to Walker Avenue. I built a studio in the backyard, nothing to be featured in *House and Garden* magazine, but ample for what I do. We—but of course I must remember now to say only *I*—have always been content here.

Today I took my usual route in the usual direction, and for the full two miles. Had I cut my walk short I would have felt guilty, which I did not want to feel. I need no additional dark feeling nowadays. And besides, after the rain the weather was pleasant and I was happy to reacquaint myself with my surroundings after being recently so inattentive to them.

Nothing out there had changed. And here inside at home, in my recent no-walking period, I'd only grown a bit older, which nothing can prevent occurring. Of course Adam is no longer here, which also we could find nothing to prevent occurring, though for a while at first we tried.

October 11, 2009

I've missed two days of walking. But then I never promised Jeffery I'd walk every single day. And I don't think he expected that, though I suppose he might prefer it. But I never did walk every single day, only three or four per week. And now that I'm walking again I'm certain there'll be some days when I'm not up to it, simply not in the mood to get out, and I'm going to try not to feel guilty about that. And then also, some days I'll be busy in the studio. I do have my work to do. And my work takes me elsewhere, for at least a few moments now and then while I'm concentrated on it, takes me away from what happened.

The new work. I started it before Adam got sick. Anyone familiar with this new series I'm developing would assume I began it in response to Adam's illness and death. But the truth—and it is admittedly an utterly breathtaking coincidence—is that I started painting dead people shortly before we knew anything at all about what was wrong with him and what his outlook was. I do not believe in ESP, or in any sort of spooky precognition hooey—there's simply no valid evidence to support any such notion—but I don't deny it feels very odd indeed that I turned my attention, rather suddenly really and, at least at first, for no conscious reason or purpose, to making portraits of the anonymous dead, this on the very eve of our learning that Adam would soon be one of them.

Not that Adam is, strictly speaking, anonymous, not at present, though of course in time we'll all be in effect anonymous, won't we? None of us, that is, will be long remembered. Our names perhaps on a list somewhere, some census record or the like, but beyond that, after some years, a few decades, a generation or two, who will have any real sense of our identities? Except perhaps in a very general, very abstract and wholly incorporeal sense, the dead are all eventually quite forgotten, each of them. Each of us. I remember talking with Adam about this years ago. We were discussing fame, or the absence of it, a point of concern for any artist of any stripe, writers of course included, anyone doing creative work, wishing it to survive its maker. We were talking about some famous person whose identity I can't now remember—and I suppose my being unable to recall this famous person's name does in some measure illustrate my point here, does it not?—Adam said to me concerning that famous person, "Yes, but his grave is going to be just as cold and dark as ours." I should make a list of such statements as this that come to me in remembering Adam, his quips often so uncommonly wise and succinct. Economical, I believe he the writer would have said, only the core idea brought forward, unmuddled by anything tangential. Though, to be honest, I've often myself found the merely tangential as engaging as whatever it's tangential to. But, yes, Adam truly was a brilliant man. I hope somehow someday to find a way to have all of his stories respectably published in book form. They deserve a place in literature, in the literature of war surely, the literature of the foolish horror of it. In a smarter world, his stories would have been provided a place while he lived. Something else I just now remember Adam saying: "Give up, give up, give up, give up, fool!" This concerning of course his attempts to have his work published, the frustration of it. But I can remember this with some amusement because he said it jokingly—with always that beguiling smile of his —yet I'm certain that, more deeply, the matter did not feel to him like a joke. One wants one's work to live. I've always thought that if worldly success is to come to artists it's best it come very late in life lest their productive years be clouded by it. But for it never to come at all . . . that is a cruelty.

A Long and Indeterminate Perambulation

I said above that I have my work to do, a commonly uttered expression. But I'd like to enter here a thought to the contrary, that the artist more likely feels it's not really the artist herself needing to do her work but the artist's work needing the artist to do it. This was true of Adam too, of both of us. We talked about it. It's the irresistible, near-palpable sense that the work itself is directing the process, making the decisions, the artist but an instrument of the work's imperatives. And I've always been entirely at ease in this, accepting my role as my work's willing and humble functionary. It's a mysterious modus operandi, to be sure, but I do not consider the matter mystical, because it's an altogether real enough phenomenon, as most artists will readily attest, little understood though it is: that our work succeeds to the extent we're attentive to the direction it requires we take.

Rain fell all during last night, and it's been dark today, dense clouds hanging near to the earth, still and damp-feeling, a bit chilly. I am at home in days of this somber tone. A lulling gloom. I went for my usual walk today with the comforting sense of being enfolded in a world at rest.

And I am ever fascinated by the objects I encounter on my way. Rubbish tossed out onto streets and sidewalks. An infinite variety of exquisite presences. Paper and plastic cups crushed by traffic—a dizzying range of color and shape—squashed Styrofoam containers, scraps of cardboard, little mangled matchbooks, fruit peels, bits of plastic and glass . . . a phantasmagoria under foot for anyone who will see.

There are moments when I feel so . . . penetrated by everything I behold around me. Penetrated. Years ago I spent some months, a couple of years actually, gathering objects I came across during my walks and using them at home in my studio as individual subjects for paintings. Wee tiny paintings, all of them, about ten inches square, so to provide for the viewer a feeling of intimacy in gazing on them, on the paintings and on the items of rubbish that were my subjects.

Some of us, I believe, are born to be observers, alert to detail typically overlooked. Beauty, I want to affirm here, is free. Beauty, truth, love. All of these are free, if you can find them.

October 13, 2009

Exactly two years now. Since Adam died. October 13. A bad-luck day. Though who can say really? It all depends on whether being alive is better than not being. And in this case good or bad luck had nothing to do with it. With his final departure itself, that is. And I respected his decision. I did then and do still. I know that in the circumstances it was the sensible action to take. I doubt poor Adam knew it was the 13th anyway, he'd become by then so detached from this world, so detached that I think physically leaving it was not a very difficult step for him to make. Two years ago. Time is so vague a thing. We have no idea what it is. If really it's anything at all. How abysmally ignorant we are about the fundamental details of existence, which as a whole we can alas comprehend no more successfully than any single feature of it. We're in darkness, even we the living.

A Long and Indeterminate Perambulation

Fog today, and not in the morning only but all day long. Beautiful. A suitably bleak ambiance on the anniversary of so dark an occasion. Fog and snow drive away color from the world. Look around, closely, and note what has happened to color on foggy or snowy days and you'll see what I mean. Color recedes. Almost, it has seemed to me, as though to hide itself away to wait for conditions more respectful of it.

A note: I seem to be adopting a slightly more casual tone here now that I've progressed some distance into this notebook. I wonder why I began more formally. Who was I trying to impress? Who will care what my tone is on these pages? It's too much work to be formal, to be so careful. I should know better than to bother. I can still be serious. I'm serious about most everything. Too serious, Adam sometimes said. But then so was he, I sometimes told him in return.

My new paintings. This new series. Portraits of anonymous dead people. And again: how odd that I began this well before we knew anything about Adam's impending death. Simple coincidence, I know, but still, how very odd it feels to think of it.

I've never asked around about this, I've never conducted a survey or come across any statistics on the matter, and I don't recall ever even talking with anyone about it, but I suspect that nearly all of us have at times found ourselves staring solemnly into the countenance of some unnamed dead person, staring, that is, at an old photograph, one perhaps of a century or more ago, of a man or woman or child who cannot any longer be alive, a person who was for a reason unknown to us directed one day to look into a camera lens and into whose eyes we now gaze in futile puzzlement.

A Long and Indeterminate Perambulation

The incomprehensible phenomenon of decease. Of life first of all, certainly, and then of leaving it, of disappearance into nonexistence, into the very same nonexistence out of which we came into being. No matter how accepting we are intellectually that life, mysterious enough in itself, ends probably in oblivion, other features of our consciousness seem incapable of reconciling ourselves with so profoundly impenetrable an occurrence. We stare at a photograph, into the eyes of someone who unequivocally is, as we contemplate this person before us, alive, yet we know that this person is now, so much time later, surely dead. The experience, if we're more than just superficially attuned to it, is not merely confusing, unsettling, but utterly ungraspable. True, we can be affected this way by paintings or drawings as well, but hardly as vividly as by way of a photograph—hence, incidentally, the shock of photography when it entered into human experience.

I've collected books of early photography, I've searched nearby library collections, I've traveled everywhere online. I've gathered together riveting images of now-dead people whose living gazes traverse the span of time between them and me so convincingly that in an altogether real enough sense, these images do, truly do, for me anyway, defy death and nonbeing.

These people are my subjects. I paint them for my own purpose, yes, which I think, to the extent I understand my purpose— purpose, another of the mysteries, for the artist and for everyone else too—is to help me sidle up closer somehow to this very eerie phenomenon I've been hashing out here concerning the dead and their continuing strangely to live by way of images made of them. And I think also that, by devoting attention to these images, or in truth to these people themselves, I'm seeking, psychologically, emotionally, to partner with them in the spanning of time, in the surmounting of death—the *trouncing* of it, I'd like to say—in which accomplishment these images are the critical instruments. I hope to infuse into my paintings the power I find in these photographs that are the inspiration for them. I hope also that I will infuse in them something of myself. And in addition, on a less complicated level, I simply like the feeling that I'm honoring these people, the dead, all of them, from all of time.

I'm reminded of something Adam always said, that no one will ever experience nothingness. When you leave, you yourself become nothing, so that of course any capacity you'd had for experience also ceases. An understanding that ironically only compounds the eagerness of our search for life in images of the dead, we in some part of ourselves refusing to believe what we know. We resist death, all of us living, even those among us wholly incapable of thought, animals who cannot comprehend its significance and its finality. Every living being resists it.

Adam dubbed me The Philosopher Painter. With that smile of his, he would call me that. I've often worried that I might be, might always have been, too much the philosopher to be given over fully to art, or maybe so much the artist that I could never be a very good philosopher. Yet I abide nonetheless as, I suppose, something of both, just as Adam said. It seems strange to me that art and philosophy are by so many thought incompatible.

Resisting death, denying it. The artist's pitiful seeking of immortality through his work. There is a wide range of other motivations for making art, true enough, some of them sage and weighty and some of them inane, altogether goofy, but trying not to die is without question prominent among them, however transparently an artist might attempt to deny it. I believe the artist's essential impulse, even if he knows it a futile one, is to document his experience, put it into concrete form in order that it will endure, never disappear. I am not a famous painter, but I've had some success in the world, and some of my best work is in safekeeping in the permanent collection of the university here where I taught for so long—though I must say, it amuses me every time I think of it that these kinds of collections are called "permanent," as though anything is. Still, the university does for at least the foreseeable future maintain in storage a good deal of work from my history as an artist, now and then bringing some of it out for exhibition, selected paintings and drawings representing stages in my lifelong passage. But, no, I cannot imagine this collection will last forever. As the decades pass, the centuries, where will be found sufficient storage room for everything that we and our descendents will have decided to save? And how far into the future can any institution live without the destructions of fire, flood, earthquake . . . all of the more or less natural disasters that in time the human-manufactured things in this world succumb to, not to mention the ever-present danger of some disastrous act of war, that enduring human lunacy. My work will in time, by one cause or another, surely disappear. But then I suppose it might be argued—laughably, I think; I in fact chuckle aloud in imagining the case being made—that a brief immortality is better than none at all. *Permanent. Always.* These words. There is nothing permanent. There is no always.

A Long and Indeterminate Perambulation

All of this notwithstanding, I continue my work anyway, which has at this point come around to painting dead people. I'll before very long be one of them. Possibly I'm only trying to cozy up to my future companions.

Two miles. I wonder whether two miles is a longer walk than I need to undertake these days. Not because I don't feel up to it physically—the two-mile walk is not a strain—but I have the sense now that I'd prefer to devote my time to other things. To my work in the studio, this new series of paintings, which I feel strangely more drawn to than to any other of my work over many years past. And maybe also to the scribbling I'm doing here in this notebook after each of my walks. I find this scribbling somehow helpful. Illuminating.

October 15, 2009

Chilly out today. I wore a jacket on my walk. And I did the full two miles; otherwise I'd have to admit to Jeffery, Dr. Jeffery, that I'd done less, and I'd like to avoid having to make that admission. Lying to him would be out of the question. I've never lied to Jeffery. And anyway I know a longer walk is better for me than a shorter one, so I did the longer one and I suppose I'll continue to do the longer one. Having a body is a bother, always having to keep it tuned, watch out for it. A nuisance. And our bodies are contrivances of only limited duration anyway. A battle lost from the very start.

A Long and Indeterminate Perambulation

The trees are finally beginning to show color this fall, some of it spectacular, the sprays of maple leaves especially, on sunny days like this one when color is not in hiding. The experience of this new fall color feels to me always like discovery, no matter that I've felt exactly this way numerous other times at the ends .of many previous summers. But yes: always as though a discovery, this radiant color. An artist revels in sensory experience. We try to make meaning of it. Maybe sometimes, in some measure, in some peculiar and incomplete way, we succeed. I now and then think so, now and then don't.

The sidewalks in this old neighborhood are richly cracked and worn, very much unlike the sterile concrete surfaces along the streets of the relatively new suburbs miles away. Someone observing my attention downward would wonder why I so often walk with my head bowed. I've taken photos of details of these sidewalks, compositions with expansive plains of varying textures, with cracks spreading through or at the edges of them, linear invasions into wide, muted color fields, or like waterways wending through desolate plateaus as seen from high above. Always these photos have been in color, oh never in mere black and white, but in color subtle yet rich, and with sometimes the sumptuous, really startling emerald green of moss growing embedded within the ancient fissures. Ancient, I say, because these walkways were lain decades ago, many of them more than a half-century ago, date-imprinted by the workmen who poured them. Some of these sidewalks were lain in place when I was a tiny child. As long ago as that. Some of them even earlier, though none as old as some parts of this neighborhood itself, which are far more than a hundred years old and at first had no sidewalks at all. People walked in the streets then, before automobiles took them.

My walk today was exhilarating. It was cold enough and dry enough that I didn't sweat, even after speeding my pace. I do not like to sweat, because then I have to shower, which takes time, and sweating means more clothes added to the laundry room, which means more time in washing and drying and ironing them. Though I do try to buy mostly clothes that need no ironing. I try to spend as little time as possible on humdrum chores. I'm increasingly aware how little time I have left now. Even if I live to be a hundred and am productive until the end, that's only twenty-five years, so very much less time than I once had.

The older we become, the more sadness we bear in our lives, all of our memories, the unhappy ones that linger on, piling up against our present. And our time here, the joy we've had, all of it nearly over, and of course irretrievable. So that the temptation for many must be to try harder and yet harder to be amused, so to keep all of that sadness at bay. But for the artist, refusing sadness would be to turn away from experience. Which would be a rebuke really, a rejection of life itself, and thus also of art and of the possibilities that inhere in it, or that we fervently hope do.

October 18, 2009

Rainy again today, as was so yesterday and the day before as well. An unusually wet fall we're having. Which interferes with my walking. Which I'm down deep glad of. But Jeffery would say the weather is no excuse, that I should exercise inside, which I really *loathe* doing and so don't. Ever. There's a level of boredom I will not endure, even for only thirty minutes. Bouncing up and down on some machine, running in place, engaging in some such goofy performance in front of the television, which, nowadays more than ever, is a toilet, or watching some silly video on the computer . . . it feels ridiculous and is insufferably boring. Insufferably, no matter what Dr. Jeffery thinks about it or says to me. So I wait until the weather is decent enough for walking. And I mean outside, where exercise is, damnit, properly taken. And where there's scenery at least.

But today the weather did finally, at the very end of the day, allow me outside, though I would rather it hadn't, even though walking is, I know, good for me, and even though it would make Jeffery happy to know I'd done it today instead of excusing myself on the basis of its being wet out and late. But enough grumbling. I walked and it was refreshing. I generally do enjoy my walks, my complaints notwithstanding. I suppose my feelings about them are mingled.

My feelings. Joy is fleeting, but sorrow lingers. It's not easy to bring an old joy back to life, not with the intensity with which it was originally experienced, but sorrow . . . a sorrow, with only the faintest effort, may be taken back into the heart. All of those years with Adam. And now this moment, and the years ahead, without him.

I believe my emotions are more fully present in my work than in my relationships with people, however close to someone I might feel. I would not like to think myself distant; I've never been accused of that, and I'm quite certain my students always knew my concern for them was heartfelt, affectionate even. Adam would tell me he saw in my eyes how much I loved him, though I cannot imagine he could ever really have known how utterly complete was my devotion, my attachment to him. And yet, no matter how true is everything I've said here, it's only in my work where all that I feel and am is most apparent, most directly accessible. It would be true for the artist, for the person who is authentically an artist, to say to someone, to the world, "You cannot know me without knowing my work. I am my work. I am not like other people."

October 20, 2009

A lovely day, a pleasant walk, and nothing more than that to set down here about it because I want instead to go immediately to something that has been rather persistently on the periphery of my thoughts recently and that today I found myself concentrated on while walking my usual route through the neighborhood. At some point I realized I was so intensely focused on pondering the matter, as though I'd been by some commanding authority assigned it, that I felt actually nonplussed.

Those who know about trees, I was thinking, know that an aged or unwell tree, an apple tree for example or a pecan tree, will often fruit far more heavily than normal in its last season before dying. I've wondered whether this new painting series I'm doing will be my last and whether my feeling so close to this work, so exceptionally fixated on it, might be in part the consequence of a subconscious realization that it could well be the last I'll do. And I've wondered whether possibly what the artist seeks is after all not his or her own immortality but simply the sending of her progeny, her work, safely into the world before she succumbs. A final bearing. I've had this thought from time to time in years past. I'm quite certain the idea is by no means original to me, that it has occurred to, and been expressed by, numerous others as well. But I've never before felt so riveted to the thought as I feel now, due presumably to my having been lately writing here about the creation of art being largely an effort somehow to thwart death, if not the death of oneself, then at least of one's work, which in point of fact is, for the artist, a kind of progeny that the art maker has issued forth. For the full duration of my walk today, the whole two miles, I've been unable to drive this tangle of inquiry from my mind.

And what anyway is the nature of this progeny? Whatever form an artist's work might take, whatever its scale, whatever the medium in which it is executed, by what name should we identify the essence of it, the property that must indispensably inhere in it?

However impermissible it is these days to say so, I believe that this essential, vital property is feeling. I'll even, here in this private journal, brave the word *sentiment*, which I rush to say is most decidedly not the same as sentimentality, which is a distortion and a debasement of sentiment.

Yes: feeling. Sentiment. Even if the content of a work of art is primarily or even exclusively intellectual—assuming that something of exclusively intellectual content, something that is entirely about idea, that is wholly without the lyrical or the sensuous, might yet be categorized as art—even concerning such a work of art as this, it was passion, even if a stringently restrained one, that made it. Commitment, caring, desire . . . some version of feeling, if only of this relatively sober sort.

Members of our contemporary aesthetic culture at its more sophisticated levels, a substantial body of them anyway, seem to shun sentiment nearly altogether. Consider recent minimalist and post-minimalist trends, the aloofness of conceptual art and the like, certain belligerent strains of performance work. Or if they don't entirely eschew it, they're at least leery of sentiment and embarrassed by it, as though fearful of experiencing any feeling at all, or, more unseemly yet, of revealing that any feeling has been felt. Adam always said that we in this era will be ridiculed in the next, that we'll be thought absurdly foolish to have banished feeling, to have adjudged it but an amusement properly consigned to the realms of the simple and uncouth.

In my long history as an exhibiting artist, no critic has ever accused me of sentimentality—my work is not mushy—but I know that what I do as an artist is born of feeling. I cannot imagine going to a canvas without feeling driving me there and informing what marks I make on it.

Yet I do sometimes wonder whether as an artist I have more feeling than skill. Given that the only point in having skill is to have enough of it to manifest feeling in one's work, it should surprise no one to learn that artists commonly wonder whether they own enough skill to accomplish that objective. And yet often the reverse is true, that the artist has wholly adequate skill but little feeling, or is perhaps inadequately acquainted with what feeling he has. I've known artists who never should have become artists, people who in neither their personalities nor their work could be discerned any level of passion that has been, or might yet be, honestly and affectingly expressed, brought out of themselves and entered into a successful work of art. Such artists typically concentrate on developing and exercising skill itself, without putting it to the purpose of manifesting feeling. Their work is therefore barren. I am increasingly convinced that some people are not only inherently incapable of making art, genuinely expressive art, but are unable even to recognize or respond to it, that such people are simply without the gene or the brain part required for doing so. Brilliant and compassionate professionals they might well be, talented engineers, physicians, wizards in discovering and describing the mechanics of the universe, generous, valiant, and noble citizens, but born without that peculiar species of sentience needed for responding to or making art.

One's work, one's progeny. A sappy analogy, it might be said. I'm not sure. The artist sending forth her work, protecting her progeny, that which has been the yield of her efforts. It does seem a nobler thing—and we naturally prefer to think of ourselves as engaged in the nobler thing—to seek for one's progeny a life far into the future than, on the other hand, to seek some puny temporary immortality for oneself. And yet, if the self, by way of one's feelings, is the essential component of one's work, if the self is thus embodied in one's progeny in this sense, then isn't the effort to secure life for one's work in truth an effort after all to secure life for oneself?

So then can the art maker ever be confident what her motives are?

A Long and Indeterminate Perambulation

I'm not at all sure it's the business of the artist to ponder such confounding matters as these, and it's certainly tiring to do so —any degree of rigorous thinking is never easy—but I seem alas compelled to it now, at seventy-five, the end in sight. And besides, Adam has officially sanctioned my propensity for speculative musing, has he not? The Philosopher Painter, he anointed me. That smile of his.

But enough.

For now.

October 21, 2009

Dear Jeffery would be proud of me: two consecutive days of walking. I wanted to go out again right away to see whether I might enjoy a stroll free of vain soul-searching—vain in both senses of the word: *futile* in the one sense (futilely inconclusive, I mean) and *self-focused* in the other. I don't in general approve of people being overly self-focused—it seems so narrow a preoccupation—yet it's true that the artist really must be deeply acquainted with and responsive to self, which after all is the well from which is drawn the expressive substance of his work.

But I do not intend to dwell again today on intangibles. No. One needs to draw into the balance an attention to the external and the concrete, the actual world beyond ourselves. Though of course some philosophers seriously, and in my view fatuously, question whether any such place actually exists—a world outside the confines of our own minds. They truly do, many of them, nutty as it seems, expend quite a lot of time and intellectual energy questioning this. And such a shame it is, goofing around on such absurdities when humanity is so desperately in need of solving problems that actually matter, problems to which inventive minds would in my unalterable opinion be far more usefully put. And yet, I cannot deny that I myself engage ofttimes in intellectual shenanigans of, I readily admit, no practical value whatever.

As I passed a house along my way during this afternoon's walk, I watched a young lady out planting mums in her front yard, she perhaps having obtained them at bargain price, its being so late now in the season. A banquet of bright color. I first noticed her from some distance and passed by slowly enough that I was able to observe her over a period of a few minutes. She was deciding where to plant these clumps of fall flowers, setting out a pot of them and then stepping back to consider its placement, positioning a second and then a third, stepping back again to consider. It occurred to me to imagine how many millions on millions of incidents of aesthetic decision-making were at that very moment taking place everywhere in the world, the busy-busy buzz and hum of the full total of aesthetic judgment being exercised in every human settlement across the globe. Leave it to the likes of me, Adam's Philosopher Painter, to think of such: at every tick of the clock, the vast numbers of us poor earthbound beasts all over this planet, some of us amateurs, some of us professionals, aspiring to the ethereal. And I, a so-called professional in the realm of aesthetics, do in the end suspect that greater sophistication does *not* necessarily bring greater satisfaction, but only greater difficulty, the decision-making of the aesthetically schooled being all the more difficult because for us nothing can any longer be simple. I'm inclined to believe that dimwits must in most regions of their lives feel satisfaction and peace more than sophisticates do. And yet we who might bear the very dubious distinction of being classified as members of that latter knighted group are ever eager to undertake, by every means we in our sophistication can bring to bear, the creation of yet more and more complication, enough finally to ensure our utter confusion concerning what actually goes on in the world and in our own murky, disquieted psyches. Some of us sophisticates (ha!) do this even to the point of debilitation. The absurdity of it.

I miss Adam. We would laugh about these things.

I remember thinking when I was younger that in old age even grief would be bearable because I would by then have grown to accept at last that nothing in human experience endures long, not life itself and therefore not the pain of it either. But now I know that grief is no more bearable at the end than at any earlier stage along the way.

On one of the corners where Adam and I usually turned as we walked together here in the neighborhood, back in the early seventies when we were participating in rallies and marches in protest of the war in Vietnam, was a house whose owner had a front-yard flower bed in the shape of a peace symbol. I remember the first time we saw it, Adam and I, how delighted we were, and how moved. I will never forget that moment.

In Buddhism we are advised to live mainly in the present moment. But the present moment passes, and then what are you left with?

A Long and Indeterminate Perambulation

October 24, 2009

I've been very much concentrated on my work in the studio these last few days, attending my paintings of the dead, or, in just as real a sense, attending the dead themselves, and so have put off walking again until this afternoon. I will behave more sensibly in future, Dr. Jeffery, I promise. Though alas my good Dr. Jeffery is all too accustomed to hearing that oft-repeated and oft-reneged-on declaration.

I cannot imagine a day more beautiful than this one. I reveled in it through every step I took over the full two miles of my walk. Bright and clear and crisp. Of course it can feel a bit deflating to realize on close consideration of the matter, deflating anyway for those unaccustomed to engaging in close consideration, that we revel in a beautiful day not because the day is perfect in any universal, absolute sense but simply because the season and the prevailing weather conditions are conducive to the wellbeing of an animal species, our own, that has evolved to function most successfully in such a setting. Bright light, moderate temperature and humidity, air neither still nor blustery, familiar, manageable surroundings . . . these among the environmental features favorable to survival, and therefore pleasant to experience. All of this notwithstanding, I see nothing foolish in feeling transported by days like this one, which we may, when we are so moved, call glorious.

Thinking again of that flowery peace symbol and of those years of war protest when Adam and I were first together, I want to record here a little of what he said concerning war, based on his experience of it and on his subsequent thinking about it. I want to commit indelibly to paper at least a few of his remarks that my recollection of that neighborhood peace symbol has brought back to me over these last few days, if only by this process to help engrave his thoughts deeper into mind so to forestall forgetting.

We're seldom finished with an experience when it's over. Hence the common wish to relive an event or to return to a place where some formative incident or traumatic ordeal occurred, so to try again to comprehend, if only viscerally, what transpired. I believe this was in part the function that Adam's writing, especially his writing about war, had for him. In his fictions he was revisiting experiences that he'd not yet fully assimilated, and that probably he never would.

Adam was a warm-humored, cheery, positive presence in this world, a man whose pleasant company was enjoyed by numerous friends and colleagues, but concerning war Adam was bitter and spoke bitterly of it. He loathed what he called "the lunacy of war" and—this another phrase he often used, angrily—the "infantile disposition" to engage in it. As well as the "tragic gullibility of the multitudes" in being hoodwinked into war by "hotheads, demagogues, charlatans, and fools."

I recall his referring vividly to human culture as ". . . but a recently formed, thin, transparent, easily rent film of civilization afloat a noxious cesspool of primeval brutal impulse." I'm certain these were the exact words of at least one portion of at least one of his frequent and richly articulated rants on the matter, and, having uttered such a string of words, Adam would always then laugh to himself at his verbal extravagance, hastening however to defend the truth of his assertion, however floridly expressed. Adam was never without his sense of humor, concerning himself first of all—I admired that about him—no matter how earnest he might be in putting forward his views about such deadly serious issues as the "mad idiocy of military enterprise," another of his commonly employed invective phrases. He had an ever-evolving repertoire of them. Many of which I've myself adopted and that I put to use on occasion even now.

I remember his often bemoaning the human capacity for technical innovation in the absence of a concomitant wisdom sufficient to guide us in how most helpfully, and peacefully, our technological advancements might serve us. "Human invention," Adam would declare, "seems only to provide ever novel ways to engage in ever more childishly bellicose and therefore catastrophic behaviors."

Religion and sports, Adam a fan of neither. I have no qualms whatever in describing Adam as a spiritual person, but the irrationality of the ordinary forms of religion was something he did not, to say it gently, approve of. "If we could lose our taste for both religion and competitive sport"—Adam thought sports like football, for example, to be products of the same combative impulse as war—"then we might have a decent shot at an honorable and agreeable experience here on Earth." And I concur. Wholly. But alas, as also Adam would now and then say, "We are after all but shaved and clothed apes newly down from the treetops."

It's all rather depressing really.

But Adam and I both felt strongly, always, that merely to accept the horrors and indignities that so reliably play out in *Homo sapiens'* farcical adventure here in this world would be cowardly and unimaginative, that it is better to seek, by whatever suitable means one might, to improve matters, even when there's faint sign of progress at hand and little hope of any to come. "Ignorance and folly are stubborn," Adam would say. "Every advance in civilization occurs only on finally overcoming, if only temporarily, the great body of inflexibly barren-brained, status-quo doltishness perpetually at work to drag down any forward movement."

Once many years ago Adam almost had a book of his war stories, his *anti*-war stories, published by a respected university press, but the university was located in a conservative region of the country and their press ultimately decided against putting it out, due, we confidently surmised, to the press's fear of displeasing their politically conservative donors and the university's equally conservative administrators, the lot of whom would no doubt have objected that the stories were anti-military. Which is exactly what these stories, brilliantly and optimistically, are.

October 26, 2009

Walking along these sidewalks, I very often think of how like others I am, all of those before me who've lived in this neighborhood, who once walked on these very surfaces I walked on today, as I have on so many other days and for so many years. Generations of walkers, most of them surely having from time to time pondered this world and our place in it in just the way I have, while they too ambled or trotted along here, their pondering as fruitless as my own. Each of us in the end equally mystified by the experience of being. By this incomprehensible universe and ourselves incomprehensibly in it, for the incomprehensibly, and agonizingly, brief time we're here. I do these days seem preoccupied by such thoughts as these. Now that Adam is gone and I'm bound soon to follow. And of course I do these days in my studio spend so much time with the dead.

Raymond is in fact coming tomorrow to see some of my dead people, now that I have a few paintings ready for him to look at. He called a few days ago about it. I'm glad to note again here how fortunate I am to have Raymond as my dealer. The Duval Gallery is the best in town, or surely one of the two or three best. No, the very best, I think. Yes. Over nearly three decades as my champion, Raymond has never faltered in his support of me as an artist. Never. And I've been through some fallow periods over the years when I could give him no work at all. Though such periods have in truth been few. And brief. I've been generally productive, working well usually. I remember saying to Raymond on one occasion when I was for some reason unable to work and therefore depressed, "I'm sorry, Raymond, the demons aren't with me at present." And then I added, "But don't worry, I'm confident they'll be along soon." And of course they did return, as they always have. *The demons* being but the old term for that range of obscure forces, more often dark than not, that impel the artist to work. Raymond now often greets me with the question, "How are your demons these days, my dear friend?" He'll then frown and inquire, "They haven't abandoned you, have they?" And then we laugh. We have a long history together.

A Long and Indeterminate Perambulation

And Raymond and I have been good for each other. Financially, yes, modestly, but otherwise too. We've been mutually supportive. We've not made each other really wealthy, but then neither of us has ever sought great wealth by way of our sojourns in the art world. I chuckle aloud at this moment to recall that in one of Adam's allegorical short stories, he vividly contrived a mean-spirited, rapacious, darkly comic character named Evil Dollar, who over a very long wicked life rendered wretched virtually everyone in his acquaintance. And it's true that wealth sometimes destroys people. Better, I think, to have only enough money and not very much more. But Raymond has made quite a good living through the gallery, and the sales of my work have certainly added significantly to my own comfort in this world. Raymond is a good man. A friend. I must be certain to tell him tomorrow how grateful I am to him and how much I respect him. Even when we feel a high regard for and much gratitude to someone, we often neglect ever to convey to that person the full extent of our feeling. I try never to be guilty of such a lapse.

Adam. I dreamed last night of him. I dreamed Adam was in the studio with me, among the new paintings I'm doing, among, that is, the other dead. I haven't been certain I'd want to note here anything about this—dreams have always felt to me too private to reveal—but I think I'd like to recount this one so to hinder its leaving me. Dreams so likely vanish. My dream had directly to do with something Adam always said about fiction writing, that imagining oneself doing something can be almost as good as actually doing it. Somewhat the way looking through a window at a beautiful scene, a sitting place on the bank of a placid lake for example, can feel very like being bodily there. Tears come now in remembering that in this dream of mine Adam stood close and said to me, "May I hug you? It might be a lengthy hug," he said. "I'll be remembering during our embrace." And then he did, in this dream, hug me. Of what followed our embrace I have no recollection. I think because in the dream our embrace was never-ending.

But dreams . . . what alas are dreams but our devoted psyches telling us stories? Stories sometimes that we crave to hear.

I want to confess to this page that grief frightens me, the prospect of being overwhelmed by it. Most experience in life can seem, in recalling it, vaporous, even illusory. Except for pain, and especially the pain of grief, which, even in memory, is all too racking.

October 28, 2009

Raymond did visit yesterday, and then I walked because Jeffery would have liked me to walk no matter what events more important than exercise might be occurring in my life, and then I walked again today. Three days consecutively I've walked. I'll tell Jeffery when I see him next. He'll think me very responsible and grown up.

I could tell when Raymond arrived that he was apprehensive about seeing these new paintings. Adam always said that beginning a new story can be like embarking on an expedition into unknown territory: you have some idea how to start off down the road, but you can never be certain beforehand what the journey farther along will be like or what you'll find when you arrive where that road will finally take you. The same is true for the painter beginning a new body of work. The artist is entering into a realm of uncertainty, where by necessity her dealer must then venture at her side, from which place he will need first to form his response to this new work and then determine how to present it. The artist, if the artist is a good artist and mature, will be as present in her new work as she was in any previous, but, within the parameters fundamentally characteristic of her, she will with this new work have set forth into an uncharted realm where others—her dealer, yes, and then also viewers, critics, collectors—might then follow, thus to be guided into a new region that will perhaps in time, depending on the vagaries, become recognizable as one of the surveyed territories comprising the wider art-world landscape. By such courses does art history progress.

But oh my. Clearly Adam was hardly the only one of us given occasionally to tangled speech. I can see him looking over at me now—his coltish smile—on reading the words I've just set down.

Almost invariably, when I see Adam I see first his smile. And for an instant it warms me, until I remember.

Raymond's visit. However understandably nervous Raymond probably was about seeing the new work, which I had rather fearfully described to him as derived of a preoccupation with dead people, he responded really quite favorably to these new paintings, speaking excitedly of their "power." Which, naturally, pleased me. *Power* is a word that both Raymond and I have always intentionally reserved for art that is exceptionally affecting, that stirs the viewer at an unusual level of intensity. He said that in his judgment this is the most profoundly moving work I've ever done. And I believe he might be right. He remarked also on the quality of spontaneity, of "unstudied directness" that he sensed in these new paintings. I told him the truth, that a while ago I'd been doing a preparatory drawing for one of the first of these new paintings and had while doing so spilled coffee on it, and that in response to that incident I'd decided simply to dispense with drawing altogether and make a beeline, without my customary charcoal-on-paper stopover, straight to the canvas, that I felt the coffee spill had functioned as a sort of permission, one I must have been seeking, to approach these paintings with greater immediacy. Again, I was elated that Raymond had sensed this change. And again I say here: my deeply felt, abiding thanks to you, Raymond.

He wants to take some of these new paintings into the gallery at some point soon so he can introduce them around to "certain interested parties," and then he wants to schedule a solo exhibition whenever I think the time is right. Raymond has never rushed me. And I don't want to rush myself either, so I'll wait until I feel ready, until I feel comfortably in control of, at ease with, this new work.

I offered Raymond a glass of wine after we finished looking at the paintings, and even a day after his visit I'm still amused in recalling the tirade—or anyway an uncharacteristically passionate harangue, I'll say it was; Raymond is typically so very reserved— that he plunged into as we spoke, about the quality of so much of the art in the galleries these days.

A Long and Indeterminate Perambulation

"I realize," he told me, "that different age groups are islands unto themselves, that rapport between one of these dominions and another far distant from it is naturally limited, and that, yes, I know, one of the obligations of age is to be forgiving of youth, but, goddamn it," he said, "I find, despite every effort to guard against it, that as I grow older I tend sometimes to regard anyone very much younger than I am as naive, shallow, and even inept. I'm not proud of this," he added, "but there it is, a confession." He remarked that he'd always admired me as an artist for not being "rule-bound," was the phrase he used. "The difference between being a slave to the rules or getting above the rules," he expounded further, his wine no doubt spurring him on, "is one of the primary differences between exercising craft and making art." (Which incidentally is what Adam often said is true for the writer as well.) And Raymond told me that my own "independence from formula and from standard expectations" had always been apparent to him in my work and that this very quality had over the years strengthened his commitment to it. But he complained that so much of the work he sees nowadays in nearby galleries is either wholly "rule-bound" or on the other hand so flamboyantly, self-consciously, and pointlessly flouting of the rules that in neither case does the artist make evident in his work any commitment to pursuing a genuinely personal direction.

Raymond appeared rather gravely disheartened by this observation. And I don't think it was the wine. Poor Raymond has in my opinion always taken art-world goings-on a little too seriously.

I told him that I seldom any longer trouble myself to become acquainted with the work of fellow artists, young or not, that in my old age I've been content to withdraw into my own interior terrain.

But I avowed I quite agree that one's attitude concerning "the rules" is of fundamental significance for the artist and, thinking of Adam, for the writer as well. I told him that, however important it is to know the rules, an artist's maturity can be measured in part by how capably he puts them aside so to go his own way, and that in the absence of rules, the all-important, the really crucial requirement is to exercise good judgment, a capacity that in youth is often not yet fully developed.

Raymond kindly pooh-poohed my speaking of being old, saying that at a full decade younger than I am he wondered how at seventy-five I managed to look so much his junior. I'm certain I blushed. I am not impervious to flattery, possibly less so now, as my dotage encroaches, than ever before. Even though Raymond is quite thoroughly gay, he is nonetheless a generous charmer of women—a habit that I think at times, as during this visit to me, falls within the sphere of charitable gesture.

I hadn't fully realized, until I made note of it just above, that I truly do not anymore have much interest in going out to see what other artists working around me are doing. I might even admit now to a degree of reclusiveness. It's true that young artists and even mid-career artists can profit, can grow in their work, by way of an interest in their context, in where they place in the world relative to others of their kind, how their work fits in, or doesn't. But at some point in the latter stages of an artist's life the obligation that feels most pressing is to devote her final energies not to the exploration of other people's worlds but to her own production, to the creation of work informed by what the artist herself has finally become in consequence of a whole lifetime of exploration, of others' worlds, yes, and of her own. We are at last the culmination of all of our striving, so that we may rightly settle confidently into ourselves alone, to make full use, without further addition or modification, of what we already are, for the compelling reason that there's little time left for making what we can of what we've grown to be.

I wouldn't want to go back to youth, to its urgency and confusion. I'm content, comparatively, in my advanced stage of life. Except, I needn't add, for backaches and the nearness of death. But, although I do not as I age grow fonder of backaches, I believe my resistance to death is diminishing somewhat, which eases my anxiety concerning mortality, and which, as though in reward for my wisdom, eases my overall tension—and thus the severity of my backaches as well. La!

As for my increased isolation from the rest of the art world, I might say this: There's a good deal of mostly laughable drama about the unsocial, sequestered artist, all of the stories that have been written about them, the eccentric artist-characters in films and plays. But, however amusing it might be to be told about such a life, it's a far more privileged thing, a richer thing, to live that life. As I increasingly do.

My Adam once joked that he was going to go out and have Leave Me Alone stenciled on the fronts and backs of all his shirts. We were much alike in this way. A pair of loners bound only to each other.

A Long and Indeterminate Perambulation

October 30, 2009

I was only beginning my walk today, barely more than a block from home, when I saw on the sidewalk across the street a little dog. He was limping, head low to the ground, clearly malnourished and suffering from who knows what range of pests and illnesses. I tried to approach the poor thing, slowly and with a few gentle, cooing murmurs, but when I was within eight or ten feet of him and he finally looked up at me, he leapt away, startled, and then scampered, painfully, it appeared, a few yards ahead along the sidewalk, from where he then turned to stare at me from that safe distance, uncertain whether I meant him harm. I tried twice more to approach, but the dog would not trust me. At last he turned onto a side street and limped away, turning two or three times to look back at me, fearfully, I think, or questioningly, before disappearing behind a street-side hedge. It was cold out this morning. This poor, ill animal is of a short-hair variety, and the days to come will be colder yet. I cannot imagine the little dog surviving through the winter, and I wish not to imagine what the end will be like for him. Our exits from this world can be hideous.

I could not continue on my walk. I turned back to home.

November 2, 2009

I looked for him, but on my walk today I could not find that pitiful creature who ran away from me a few days ago. In my time of life, looking back, as people in this shocking time of life are given sometimes to do, I am tormented by those occasions when I could have, but did not, relieve suffering. The suffering of animals—I'm thinking of that little dog; I might have tried harder to capture it, to help—and of people too. I can think of no occasion ever in my life when I caused suffering intentionally, but I know that I have sometimes neglected to relieve it. Because I've been too busy to console someone. Or too uncertain whether I should. Because I've chosen not to support humane causes when actually I could have managed to do so. Because I've at times not been sensitive enough to perceive the suffering near me. And yet perhaps I shouldn't accuse myself of being all too terribly stone-hearted. Years ago at school, looking through the window one very frigid winter day at a group of pigeons huddled together on the exterior windowsill of a building across the way, I remarked to a fellow teacher on how awfully cold the birds must have been, that the university might at no real expense construct some sort of rude over-wintering shelter for them, whereupon my colleague joked that I seemed afflicted with "empathitis." I was quite aware that pigeons can endure all but the most extreme cold. I knew they were in no real danger of freezing to death. I'd only been imagining the birds' discomfort. Empathizing, yes. I believe I recall responding to this woman more testily that I should have: "Compassion that does not extend to animals is a flimsy, half-assed compassion," I think I told her. But I cannot now recall what words on the matter, if any at all, were exchanged between us afterward.

Adam and I ceased eating animals many, many years ago. And then always after wondered why we'd been so long in coming to that decision. The horrible suffering caused by the indefensibly brutal treatment of food animals. And the unceasing, systematic delivery of cruel death. We'd been simply blind to it. I wonder now how people can become aware of these horrors and yet continue blithely to contribute to them. I would once have thought this a failure to comprehend fully what misery they're causing. But I attribute it now to a failure of empathy. A refusal to care.

I suppose too that the common notion we're special, that we're fundamentally so superior to animals that their suffering is of no consequence, contributes to our often hideous mistreatment of them—a behavior hardly consistent with the "superior" sensibility human beings so commonly ascribe to themselves relative to other creatures.

Of course I'm careful about expressing these thoughts to others lest I provoke only ire. Some people can become so prickly and defensive over the matter.

The temperature today was barely above freezing, unseasonably cold, but the sun was bright and the air still, so that it felt warm out. Blazing color on this clear, crisp day.

November 7, 2009

I skipped four days of walking. I won't tell Dr. Jeffery about this. Though I think he would not be surprised. He knows my resolve concerning exercise is weak. But, however much Jeffery might be disappointed in me, I acknowledge that I'm disappointed in myself as well. I will try to do better. I always try to do better. At least I did walk today finally, despite the nippy weather—low, dark clouds and an inhospitable, cutting breeze. But I was well bundled up against the chill and so was comfortable enough. Bodily, that is, though not, I need to say here, in spirits. I've been grieving more lately than usual. Possibly my sadness over the heartbreaking sight of that little dog the other day triggered it anew. Not that my grief these days needs any prompting. It comes over me in battering waves, receding for a while only to assail me again as though of its own hostile intent. It hasn't been very long really, since he left. I'm certain it's normal that I haven't let him go. And a normal, ordinary grief is undoubtedly how mine would be characterized by those psychology professionals—and oh so admirably objective they are— who study how humans mourn their losses. I am not consoled. My grief is my own, it is unique to me, and it is unbearable, however goddamn "normal, ordinary" someone far outside it might judge it to be.

As for the consolation of religion, "Cowards and fools cling to their numbing mythologies," is what one of Adam's characters tells another in one of his stories. And of course this is Adam himself speaking through one of his made-up people. We're so unwilling to accept death, he wrote somewhere else in that story, that in our cemeteries we build, if we can afford to, little, or massive, stone domiciles where our dead will reside as though they were yet alive and will be forever, as though death never happened to them, or as though its happening had been inconsequential. I think perhaps it's not that the human psyche can't accept someone's departure from among us but that we're unable fully to grasp the stark nature of it. We do not comprehend the finality of death when it occurs, so we behave as though it simply doesn't. In my head I understand that this is so of us, most of us, that we deny the reality of death, and in my heart I understand why. My dear Adam remained rational to the end. No fantasizing. No temptation to do so. I hope I can honor him by doing as well. But I feel most of the time that I don't even know how to be old—it seems so foreign a place to be—so how could I possibly know how to die? Although clearly our dying does not, alas, need our knowing how to do it.

Adam did, naturally, experience some anxiety as he grew nearer death, but what he told me about it is that he took comfort in knowing death would come soon to put an end to his anxiety about its coming so soon. How remarkable. Often in the midst of my mourning, as now, I'm warmed in recalling the humor that Adam would bring even to so dark a matter as this. And his smile.

It does comfort me to understand that the life we experience is after all only a mechanism.

A mechanism like all others in the natural world. Like the way trees spring up from seed and grow tall, shed their leaves in fall and generate new ones in spring, drop their dead branches after they're no longer of use to them, heal themselves if damaged by lightening or wounded by falling neighbors, and then, if they survive long enough against fire and windfall and disease, they in time die at the limits of their endurance, collapse onto the forest floor, disappear into earth and air, other trees then springing up in their places. And so on through time, all details of the process overtaken by other details forever.

It comforts me to know that our lives are ultimately of no greater matter in this indifferent universe than any other such phenomena occurring within it. It is a solace to know that our emotions, like the blood cells in our veins, the nerves at the surface of our skin, are but a feature of the mechanisms we are, that our feelings are only the products of an arrangement of molecules in our brains, these chemicals that compel us, that make our lives matter to us, that can make experience feel like transcendence.

A bleak assessment, this, nearly everyone would say. Hence the near-universal imagining of more agreeable possibilities.

Regardless of what might be the truth obtaining among these issues, if indeed any such creature as truth obtains here at all, what else are we to do in this life but what we feel we must?—whatever the source of that feeling. And then at last to sleep a child's untroubled sleep forever.

Adam would say of his stories that they're idea-driven, lingering on such perplexities as I've touched on here. He would say to me in whisper that he was possibly more philosopher than story teller. "The Philosopher Painter and The Philosopher Scribbler," he'd say of us. Adam thought narrative useful only as the armature on which the more gripping aspects of a fiction might be built. "Story alone is mundane," I remember his saying. "And no need troubling to make them up; there are millions of them out there everywhere—at the Rite Aid," he'd say, "in the home of your neighbors next door, in your own family, in your lifetime of recollections, in what people reveal in the most casual conversation. Story is the easy part, and the least interesting one." But, if Adam was not very much enthralled by story, he did grow very close to his characters. He said he sometimes felt more intimately associated with them than with most of the real people he knew, in that his made-up people had their whole existence within his very self, ". . .

whereas 'real' people are out there in the world at comparatively a very great distance." Except for me, he was always at pains to be certain I knew. As of course I did. I needed no verbal assurance. I knew.

November 12, 2009

I did walk this afternoon, all two miles. But I've been deplorably remiss. Deplorably. I let four days go by without even stepping outside. Four days. I feel like a downcast sinner, confessing unpardonable wickedness to this page. And I know, I do know, that too many stretches of inactivity could undermine my good health. Jeffery has warned me, repeatedly. I fully understand this.

But I was occupied. Busy in the studio. I love my neighborhood, and I love walking in it, truly I do, but there are periods when I can allow nothing short of emergency to interrupt my concentration. The work must at times be my only concern.

And I've been thinking that it's as true for me as it was for Adam that the characters that figure in our work, in his fictions and in my paintings, have seemed more real than the people known to us in this realm of the flesh. My dead people, these portraits I'm doing now. Seldom do we who are alive stare as long and as searchingly into the faces of our living acquaintances, even intimate ones, as I do into the faces of my dead subjects, first their faces in old photographs and then those faces during the long and delicate process of seeking to bring these people alive again on canvas.

But, however earnestly devoted I am to this new body of work, however driven to realize my expressive ambitions in the exploration of it, I can only wonder sometimes, even during the very act of brushing paint onto canvas, why I trouble myself doing it. We human beings are stupidly, or perhaps psychopathically, voraciously, crowding this world beyond capacity, using it up and fouling it as though by actual intention to destroy it utterly and thus eventually ourselves as well. So who, in the absence of a posterity, does the painter paint for, the writer write for?

A foolish question. I'm embarrassed to have asked it here. The true artist paints for herself. True artists have always worked primarily for self, even when working ostensibly for others, as on commission, and even when it's been all but certain no posterity would exist to regard the work being done. We work for the experience of working. The prospect that what the artist does will be valued by others does undeniably matter to her—renown in the present, and perhaps even immortality, if only, as I've said, a temporary one, her work thereby living on into at least some part of the future. But, as she is working, if she is a true artist, she is always in that moment working for herself.

That society honors artists, when it does, while they live or after, I think is good. But I think it not very good that only very few are honored, the few who've become renowned, sometimes for reasons not entirely germane to their work itself—scandal, personality, good fortune—while most others, some of them more deserving of honor than the famous, are thought little of, if ever they're thought of at all. But then of course the behavior of human beings is ofttimes preposterous.

As for example, speaking of the preposterous, the artist's desire for immortality, however loosely defined and however limited in duration, by way of one's work. As well as the lame rationalizations we put forward in an effort to justify our desiring it. Take for example, as even I the ever so rational Painter Philosopher have previously posited on these pages, our insistence that we wish only, altruistically, to secure life for our progeny. How transparent a song and dance is that little subterfuge, or anyway is often felt to be. (Let it be noted how honorably I enter here into the realm of self-rebuttal.) Dead, it might more reasonably, and certainly less tortuously, be maintained, is dead, period. And yet we do strive to live, by whatever fanciful means we can conjure, via religion, art, reputation, or by various other modes of inventive, magical thinking. What the human animal lacks in courage required to face reality, he makes up for in dazzling arrays of illusion that prevent his having to do so.

But of course, given how terrifying this life ultimately is, how harsh and lonely, and then the ever more terrifying prospect of leaving it, I suppose it would be cruel indeed to blame ourselves for wishing to be by one means or another transported. Adam has said that "all religion is bullshit. Coming to grips with that truth can be the beginning," he would say, "of a sound intellectual life." And I quite agree. But we are born into this world like children waking afraid in a strange house, in a strange land, with only strangers all around us. And we never grow at ease here. We feel all our lives bewildered and forsaken. Until I grew old and accepting of my abject ignorance concerning the nature of this life and of this place where we live it, I would grow near to despair. But now at seventy-five I see that despair is pointless, an indulgence of youth, a version of self-pity. I find that in my old age there's no time left for that sort of thing.

I've been in recent days resisting a thought that has been ever so gingerly, though with unabated insistence, impinging on my consciousness: the possibility of including Adam in this new work based on photographs of the dead. And now that I've at last allowed the idea entrance into mind, I'm startled every time I think of it. How very strange that in coming to this series I never once consciously considered including Adam. But of course the others are strangers to me, the strangers, as I say above, whom we all live, or have lived, among. The anonymous dead. How could I admit my beloved Adam into such a gathering?

I think sometimes that, when all consideration of the matter is exhausted, the only thing worth learning about life is that we must very soon leave it. A truth obvious and uncomplicated—though the catch, I suppose, is that, if it is uncomplicated, we cannot feel it to be so.

It was cold out today.

November 16, 2009

Alas another three days without walking. And therefore also without writing here in my walk-days journal.

The afternoons are darker now, the sun timid.

Even though I've missed a few days, and even with Dr. Jeffery's admonishments sounding in my ears, today I walked only barely half of my usual two miles. I feel lately more and more focused on the work and less and less concerned about worldly matters outside it. But of course this is nothing new for me, a familiar territory I enter from time to time during certain crucial periods of involvement (*evolvement*) with my painting.

Still, despite its being chilly and dark today, my short walk was, I admit, invigorating. I always do find my walks pleasurable, if only I can get myself out to begin them—which, again, I seem lately to be having increasing difficulty doing.

The sun. "Timid," did I say? A rather too hokey way of putting it. Though were I a poet from a bygone romantic era I could easily have gotten by with so blatant a pathetic fallacy, so mushy a trope. How fashions in art do change. And how vigorously do practitioners of the current fashion, in the current moment, defend its narrow dictums. Adam and I once discussed my making drawings based on characters and incidents in his short fictions, these images to accompany the stories as integral features of them. But so many of his friends in the Creative Writing Program at the university frowned on the concept that we finally put it aside in the realization that publication of the stories and images together would be unlikely. It's apparently a feature of the currently fashionable attitude toward fiction writing that a story as it appears on the page must not be sullied by the presence of visual images, that doing so somehow undermines what all the academics these days call "the fictional dream." Never mind the many, many centuries—all of those ancient texts on parchment—of prominently placed visual representations of what is being conveyed in words, this clearly to permit the reader literally to see what is being written about. And in more recent literary history we have the illustrated works of William Blake, Thackeray, Trollope, Thomas Hardy, Hermann Hesse, Kipling, Vonnegut . . . Probably at some point in the next century, illustrated stories will again be all the rage. It's quite maddening, and harmful really, these narrow, fashion-bound conceptual restrictions on art, whatever the medium. Every moment in the history of art and literature has its myriad sacred rules, numbers of them doomed to scorn and rejection in the very next moment to come.

The sun, however, does at least *seem* timid on these near-winter days, as though intentionally veiling itself behind dense gray overcast, with but the faintest suffused yellow glow betraying its unwilling presence. A lovely sight. Beautiful—whatever that means.

I will confess here a dark thought. The phrase, *a beautiful day*. So common an expression this is. And yet, whenever I myself utter it, which I do as often and as casually as anyone else, I always feel at the same time, beneath that cheery remark, a subtle unease. A beautiful day is on the surface reassuring, it's true. A beautiful day inspires in us the sense that all is well in this our benign world. But I am never without the sense in addition that however beautiful a day is, that day is also incomprehensible, uncontrollable, and oblivious to me. Which observation can be terrifying if dwelled upon. But which also, paradoxically, makes such a day even more stirring yet, even more beautiful.

A Long and Indeterminate Perambulation

November 23, 2009

Jeffery will kill me. He'll give me that unnerving accusatory stare. That look of impatience, of vexation, chagrin, pique. It withers me when he does this. And yet I do so often disobey him nonetheless. Not because I don't regard seriously his instructions, but probably because I'm weak. I have puny resolve. Which—oh, my—sounds rather like an actual medical condition, and in fact might well be one: chronic puny resolve. If only there were a pill for this malady. Or maybe there is. I'll ask Jeffery. The man knows all.

But I won't tell him I neglected my walks for a whole week. I don't have to tell Dr. Jeffery everything. It is my impulse to do so, to confess to him each of my egregious transgressions, unreservedly, but I don't have to.

I did the full two miles this morning. And in a cold drizzle too. Not so bad. Bracing really. We'd had a hard, steady rain during the night, and I always love seeing afterward how the water flowing down from sloping driveways or through the gutters has left little piles of leaves arranged almost as though in sheaves, how the motion of the water can be discerned in these patterns it creates as evidence of its passing.

These assemblages of leaves, these little monuments, accidents of nature though they be, appear disconcertingly like objects born of human intention. But of course human intention is itself, in the view of some of us, an accident of nature. A judgment that, however off-putting it apparently is for many, I personally find entirely satisfying. I've anyway, in all my seventy-five years, stumbled across no plausible reason to conceptualize the matter differently.

I've waited until the end of this entry to record that Raymond called to ask whether I will allow him this soon to take perhaps a trio of my new paintings for the gallery. Not yet to sell, but only, as he said in these always amusing words of his, to "whet appetites," a phrase he has often repeated and that clearly he enjoys using, one that is delightfully expressive of good Raymond's keen enthusiasm for promoting his artists. And for Raymond, seeking attention to his artists is by no means purely a dollars and cents matter, or even primarily that, but has actually more to do with what I consider a very beautiful and laudable generosity that is characteristic of him, his seeking recognition for the artists he's taken on. Raymond's devotion to us is moving, really heartwarming, which is in part why we, all of his artists, love him and are loyal to him.

Raymond is so unlike many other dealers. Adam, as well as other fine writers in our acquaintance, complained about the current loutish state of publishing in this country, that publishing houses are run now by money interests, not by people committed to literature. They're all looking for the next bestseller, which means they're looking for work that will have the broadest possible appeal, which means consequently that they're likely to publish mostly drivel, sometimes nicely crafted drivel, but drivel nonetheless. Anything too genuinely literary, perhaps too intellectual for the masses or too unconventional, which is what a number of Adam's longer things are like, is put aside. "'But publishing is a business,'" Adam would quote their declaring in defense. A business. And yet the truth is this: that publishing books with an eye only to make money is base hackwork, just as are the products of writers who write with predominantly the same objective in mind. Both behaviors are almost exclusively mercenary and are therefore, in contrast with honorable literary expression and the publication of same, ugly and shameful, or at least undignified. And many commercial art galleries, many more than is realized by the lay public, operate with similarly unsavory purpose.

An art gallery that is of consequence beyond simply sustaining itself financially doesn't choose work based on the likelihood of its appeal to buyers—or collectors, to speak of them more graciously—but on the gallery director's informed response to the work, the degree to which he is affected by it, his convictions concerning the work's merit, its inherent expressive power. In a gallery that functions as more than merely a money-maker, the gallery owner's enthusiasm and respect for the work is primary. Only if he is personally committed to the work will he set about committing to sell it. What matters, ethically, morally—spiritually? —is which of these commitments is foremost. No seriously respectable art gallery, and no respectable publisher either, is in business only to do business.

Raymond has even in some cases actively endeavored to discourage potential purchasers. Of my own work and of others' too. This because selling simply is not itself the paramount objective at The Duval Gallery. He seeks always to place his artists' work in worthy collections, whether private, corporate, or museum, instead of surrendering it into the possession of anyone able to wave at him the requisite amount of cash so that they can display a painting, or a sculpture or drawing or print, like a souvenir, an emblem of cultural awareness taken home with them from some giddy weekend foray into the wacky world of the arts. Raymond is solemnly protective of his artists' long-term careers, indeed considers himself a builder of them.

He and his young assistant—and oh my goodness how very, very young she did appear to be, and how youthfully venerating was her disposition concerning my ancient but only minorly venerable self—he and this eager child came yesterday and took two of my new paintings back to the gallery. They'd wanted three, and well more than three were ready to leave me, but in the end I allowed Raymond only the two. We've after all come this far a bit sooner than I'd anticipated so that I wasn't yet fully prepared to part this early with even two of them. Nonetheless, I suppose it is by now time to send some of these paintings, these deceased, out into the world, this world they once departed, believing their withdrawals permanent, but that they will now occupy once again, however unexpectedly. I imagine them numbed by surprise.

December 1, 2009

I've decided to make no further apology here for my failure to exercise. Until today I hadn't walked in over a week. I have, damn it, other things to do. If Jeffery doesn't ask outright, I won't voluntarily confess anything to him. If he does, and if I can't lie, which probably I won't be able to do, I'll just summon, from *some*where, the courage to tell him I've been too busy in the studio and that sometimes I'm simply incapable of dividing my time and concern between this work that is vitally important to me and what seems by comparison a frivolous interruption of it. Still, I *will* try to walk now and then. And I *will* try to do it more often than seldom. I walked finally today. Despite its being too cold to be out, I did walk. I think possibly only to salve my guilty conscience.

December 6, 2009

Raymond called to say that response to the paintings he took into the gallery has been "even more enthusiastic than expected." Evidently my dead people appeal. I needn't remark that I'm pleased. Naturally I am.

Yet I feel strangely in the background, as though I were in truth rather little involved in this phenomenon—of these paintings coming into existence, of their being taken into a gallery, seen there, and of people responding to them. My very strong sense is that my subjects, these dead people themselves, are the operable force, not I who only, though I hope with skill and compassion, transferred their likenesses to canvas. And I'm fully at ease in this, as though all is as should be. Of course artists often do report feeling this quite perplexing sense of being somehow outside their work, as if the work simply doesn't really need them, as if it creates itself, so that artists can feel eerily irrelevant, possibly the way a mother can feel increasingly unneeded as a child mysteriously develops its own identity and grows more independent of her. But this new work, my portraits of the dead, perhaps because these people seem to me, as I work with them, so like vital, alive forces, it causes me to feel even more than normally the merest ancillary in the production of these paintings.

Raymond has not yet officially offered my two paintings for sale, though he did divulge to me that interest has been clearly expressed by several parties, including especially a couple who've bought my work in the past and whose collection has grown—I'm pleased for them and for me too—rather important over the years. We haven't even discussed price yet. Raymond hinted, gently so not to make me feel rushed, that we need soon to discuss our doing a solo exhibition of this new work. I agree and will make my agreement clear to him next time we speak.

And yes, yes, I did walk today. I walked.

It was cold. But I do love these still, soundless, dark days, this otherworldly hush that can be so spellbinding. A uniformly dense gray sky today . . . and the twisted branches of trees silhouetted black against it like viscous ink on dusky paper.

I'm aware—and I accept it, not happily, but not resentfully either, though it did once, in my youth, anger me—that eventually all of this, all that we love, all that we know and are, will disappear into some gaping and indifferent black hole in space. All gone. To nothing, or anyway to some equivalent of nothing. The trick, which I wish were known to all, and which I must remind myself of now and again, is not to fret over it, not to fulminate against the evanescence of existence, but to surrender to this feature of it. Which of course does not release us from the obligation to conduct ourselves decently in the present moment, however brief we know this moment is bound to be, for the moment we have is real enough for us and does therefore matter, to us. What else, after all, do we have?

All to nothing, ourselves included. And yes, surely we must in wisdom accept this inevitability. But I remember Adam remarking when he became ill that people who are not much distressed by the prospect of dying must have a relatively weak sense of the self, so that they feel lower than ordinary levels of anxiety and sorrow on anticipating its extinguishment. He said he'd known people like this. As have I.

Concerning the extinguishment of self, I shall utter here, unashamedly, surely the most oft-spoken cliché in the entire history of human pondering: that time speeds by, life goes quickly. And of course it does. It goes so quickly that one might at any point at all in one's life think of it as practically over already. And yet I smile to myself in wonder concerning my nonetheless looking beyond, into a future in which I will not be present. Why do I find it satisfying to imagine others living in my house, enjoying the amenities, however modest, that we created here for ourselves: the kitchen Adam and I remodeled years ago, the deck at our back door, so pleasant a place to sit in good weather, the better lighting we installed in the attic, the bookshelves in the den . . . I like to think of them, my successors in this house, even though they'll surely never think of me, at least not by name, not with an awareness of my specific identity. I like to think also of my predecessors here, whoever they might have been, imagining how they used these rooms, where they sat, what they spoke of among themselves. I believe that as a species we're given to an awareness of, even to an investment in, continuity, life before us and life after us. A behavior that, among other useful functions, does aid somewhat in moderating the grievous offense of individual demise.

Our heroes in the arts—composers, artists, writers long dead —can seem to us yet alive, can seem bound to live always, because, by way of their work, they live in us. But they too are dead. They did die. As will, at some point in time to come, all that is known of them. As well as all they did—which can seem to us the most unfathomable kind of death, and the most tragic.

Earlier on these pages I mused about how my painting portraits of the dead causes these dead to seem alive, and I wondered as I wrote whether, since this is so, I should include Adam among my subjects. I've come to no decision. It has always been my habit, when in quandary, not to force conclusion of a matter but to step away from it for a while and allow the issue to resolve as though by its own interior energies. I have numerous endearing photographs of Adam, but whether I should take one of these into the studio to work from it as I've worked from photographs of my other dead, those who've come to me as unknowns . . . this question seems somehow not to have found its footing for me. I sense no movement toward resolution. I am unable to know what I should do.

Whenever I'm out now I am automatically, habitually, on watch for that little dog, though I realize there's no likelihood I'll see it again. I doubt even that it could have survived until now. Was it afraid in its last days? We wonder what emotions, what thoughts might be swirling about in the heads of little animals. And we, most of us, assume that, whatever might be the exact nature of their thoughts, of their impressions of the world and their concerns, they must surely be inconsequential. But I suspect that our assuming the thoughts and feelings of animals to be insubstantial has more to do with our over-estimating the importance of our own.

December 14, 2009

Today, snow and ice. Not nice. To walk in. So I didn't.

But then I've not walked in some days. For which I do not apologize.

I write here today without having walked. I suppose I'll take up my walking again at some time later on. One day when the weather is better, in the spring perhaps, months from now.

Christmas is near. The spending season. On these cold winter days, in the boorish commercialism of this allegedly sacred holiday period, I am warmed in remembering the words my Adam always called out on the twenty-sixth, the morning after, as unto the heavens: "Ah, Christmas! The joyous season is thank god over for another year praise Jesus!" His smile. His laugh.

Raymond and I have scheduled my solo exhibition for next fall. October, I think it is. By which time I'll have more than enough of these paintings. We're excited.

An eternal rest as reward for our work on earth? What a bore, eternal rest. A little break would do, and then back to our labors.

E N D

— A Long and Indeterminate Perambulation —

Photo: Ashley Drew

Robert McGowan's work as an artist is in numerous collections internationally, including among others, Bank of America, Bank of Korea, Cranbrook Art Museum, and the Smithsonian American Art Museum.

His images have appeared in and on the covers of literary journals in America and abroad, including *American Literary Review, BRAND* (UK), and *dotdotdash* (Australia). His essays and short stories, the latter frequently set in the art world, are published in over five dozen prominent literary journals in America and abroad, including *The Black Herald* (France), *Chautauqua Literary Journal, Connecticut Review, Etchings* (Australia), *The Louisiana Review, New Walk Magazine* (UK), *The Savage Kick* (UK), and *South Dakota Review,* have been four times nominated for the Pushcart Prize, and have been several times anthologized.

McGowan is the author of the story collections, *NAM: Things That Weren't True and Other Stories* (Meridian Star Press (UK), 2011) and *Stories from the Art World* (Thumbnail Press, 2011), a collection of eight short fictions set in the art world and accompanied by various series of McGowan's own visual work. This year will also see the releases of his collections *Happy Again at Last: Life in the Art World* (Shanti Arts Publishing, 2012/13) and *South Main Stories* (Downtown Productions, 2012).

Robert McGowan lives in Memphis, Tennessee, USA.

His website is **http://robert-mcgowan.com**

Made in the USA
Lexington, KY
13 January 2013